D0091839

On the Frontier
With Mr. Audubon

Walker

On the Frontier with Mr. Audubon

By Barbara Brenner

Drawings by Fred Brenner

Boyds Mills Press

Text copyright © 1977 by Barbara Brenner
Drawings © 1997 by Fred Brenner

Published by Caroline House
Boyds Mills Press, Inc.
A Highlights Company
815 Church Street
Honesdale, Pennsylvania 18431
Printed inthe United States of America

Library of Congress Cataloging-in-Publication Data
Brenner, Barbara.
  On the frontier with Mr. Audubon / by Barbara Brenner
[xxx]p.
Originally published by Coward, McCann, Inc., N.Y., 1977
Summary: Audubon's young apprentice describes the experiences he shared with his
master during their eighteen month trip down the Mississippi studying and drawing
the birds they found along the way.
ISBN:
1. Mason, Joseph—Juvenile literature. 2. Audubon, John James,
1785-1851—Juvenile literature. 3. Naturalists—United States—
Biography—Juvenile literature. 4. Artists—United States—
Biography—Juvenile literature [1. Mason, Joseph. 2. Audubon, John
James, 1785-1851. 3. Naturalists. 4. Artists] I. Title.
QH31.M28B73 598.2'092'4[920]   LC
Library of Congress Catalog Card Number:

First Boyds Mills Press edition, 1997
The text of this book is set in 12-point Times.

10 9 8 7 6 5 4 3 2

CONTENTS

To Fred, who embodies the Audubon spirit

Part One
On the Flatboat

October 11, 1820
The Beginning

My name is Joseph Mason.

Most likely you never heard of me. Or of my teacher, Mr. John James Audubon. He is a painter around these parts and teaches drawing to young persons like myself. He also works at the museum here in Cincinnati, where his job is preparing birds for the museum's displays.

Mr. Audubon has a regular passion for birds. He has a notion to paint *every bird* in America and make a big book or portfolio of them for folks to marvel at. Right now he is planning a trip down the Ohio and Mississippi rivers to search for birds to paint. And now here is where Joseph Mason comes into the picture. John James Audubon has asked me to go with him!

I am to help Mr. Audubon find bird specimens and to do

other chores for him as he may need me. In return, he will provide my board and also teach me drawing. I hope to be a painter when I grow up, but while Mr. Audubon's specialty is birds, mine is plants and flowers.

Both Mr. Audubon and I like nothing better than to hunt and fish and tramp through the woods; we are much alike in that. I think that may be why Mr. Audubon chose me to go on this trip with him.

I aim to set down in this journal all that happens to us on this trip. I shall do it as truly and faithfully as I can, because I know that although Mr. Audubon is only a poor painter now, someday he will be famous. Then people will want to know all about how he made his bird paintings. And maybe they will also want to know something about Joseph Mason and this frontier journey.

October 12
All Aboard

At half-past four this afternoon we stepped aboard a flatboat bound for New Orleans. The dock was crowded with boxes and bales, as well as with voyagers and their families come to see them off.

We made a goodly crowd ourselves: there was Mama and Papa, Mr. Audubon, Mrs. Audubon, and Victor and John, who are the Audubons' sons. There was a lot of hugging and kissing all around, which embarrassed me no end. I got caught by both ladies, who patted and fussed at me as if I were a boy of six instead of an almost full-grown lad of thirteen.

Papa, however, treated me like a man. We shook hands, and he talked to me earnestly. Told me to work hard and to pay heed to what Mr. Audubon can teach me. I will do that. I think Papa would be proud for me to become a painter. He values all forms of culture highly.

Seemed like before we knew it, the crew was casting off. A few last words and our families were hustled ashore. By five o'clock we were drifting out into the channel—on our way.

Now it's late. Way past my bedtime at home. I'm in the cabin of the flatboat, sitting with Mr. Audubon. We are both writing in our journals.

I guess I'm lucky. Not many thirteen-year-old boys get the chance to travel down the Ohio and Mississippi all the way to New Orleans. Scares me a mite, though. Never was this far from home before. I keep thinking of my mother and father. Mama's cheek was wet with tears when she kissed me this afternoon. And Papa suddenly looked so old and frail. . . .

I wonder when I'll see them again. I asked Mr. Audubon how long he figured we'd be away. Maybe six months, maybe a year, he says. Mr. Audubon says he misses his family already. He brought with him a painting that he made of Mrs. Audubon, whose name is Lucy. He says his wife is his best friend. "She eez my bast fraind." That's the way he said it. Mr. Audubon has an odd way of speaking. He's French, I believe.

We're going to sleep now. Mr. A. says we shall sleep on deck. The air is better out there, he says. We have buffalo robes to roll ourselves in, so we shouldn't be cold.

And so to bed. More about this boat tomorrow, when it's light enough for me to see.

October 13
The Flatboat

Sun in my eyes woke me this morning. Mr. Audubon was already up and off somewhere. I sat on the deck for a spell, getting a closer look at my new home. I've seen many a flatboat from the shore, but this is the first time I've seen one from the deck.

A flatboat is really a large raft with sides. It's about forty feet long. Both ends are squared off, and it has some cabin space as well. Most of the passengers stay on deck. Many of them are taking their livestock down the river to sell or to trade, so the deck looks like a regular Noah's Ark or a traveling barnyard. *Smells* like a barnyard, too. Can't hardly get a whiff of the river for all the pig and chicken smell.

This kind of boat has no sails or steam, so we're at the mercy of the wind and the river current. On a brisk day we can travel up to fourteen miles or so. But if there's no wind, we have to sit like a big, clumsy cow in a mudhole, until the breeze or current takes us again.

We got stuck like that this afternoon, which sorely provoked Mr. Aumack, our captain. Mr. Aumack is a young man, but he has an old face that is weather-beaten and leans to sour expressions. When he is angry or upset, as he was when the boat stopped moving, his face turns color. It sometimes goes red and sometimes as purple as an iris. I couldn't take my eyes from him at supper. Felt quite shy when he caught me staring.

The other people on the boat seem used to our slow progress. The children run and play on the deck as if they were at home, while their mamas work at their washtubs or sit knitting in the sunshine. Some of the passengers are squatters, going down river to find new homes. Others are tradespeople with goods to sell. They will set up shop whenever the flatboat stops at a town. And when they have nothing more to sell, they will leave the boat and begin the long walk home.

The sailors are a rough crew. Whenever a keelboat or steamboat passes us, they line up on the side of the boat to yell and cuss at it. The sailors on the other boat do likewise, and everyone seems to make good sport of it.

Mr. Audubon laughed when he saw me listening to that

coarse talk. He say's it's a custom, called blackguarding. The game is to call the loudest and worst insults. Some of the passengers join in, too. But not Mr. Audubon; he is too much of a gentleman for that. He has fine manners and always speaks in a soft, polite voice, although he looks like the roughest frontiersman. He dresses in boots and buckskins and wears his hair long, down to his shoulders. With his beard and his piercing blue eyes, he is quite handsome, save for his teeth, which are rotting.

We have our meals in the cabin with the captain and crew. Here, too, I learn a few words I would not hear in Sunday school. There is a lot of whiskey drinking, even in the morning. Mr. Seeg, one of the crew and our cook, seemed quite drunk by noon. He is a big, burly fellow and a bully with the whiskey in him. I will stay out of *his* way.

Mr. Audubon and I spent a good part of this day sitting on a deck sketching. The rest of the time we were busy oiling our guns and getting ready for our first hunting expedition, which will take place tomorrow. And Mr. Audubon told me more about his plans for this trip.

Now here I got a surprise. It seems that Mr. A. hasn't a penny to his name. He has got us passage on this boat with the promise that we will supply game for the captain and his crew! So I shall be *hunting*, if not *singing*, for my supper. And for everyone else's, too.

Now about the birds for Mr. Audubon's paintings. He needs examples of every species of bird common to these parts, including those which have never been named in other bird books. He calls these nondescripts—which means that no one has described them. Mr. A. has a book with him by a Mr. Alexander Wilson, which he uses as a guide. But Mr. Audubon hopes to include in *his* bird book many species that Mr. Wilson does not picture. If I find a new species Mr. Audubon says he may name it for me. Mason's hawk! Mason's flycatcher! Even Mason's eagle! How fine that sounds. I shall look sharp for new birds, you may be sure.

We are all ready. Powder dry, boots greased, guns in order. Tomorrow we start hunting in earnest. I hope that game is plentiful, otherwise two artists and the crew of this flatboat will be going hungry.

And so to bed on deck, where we sleep on stretched buffalo hides. The cows and pigs are never very far away, but it is better out there than in the cabin, which is always full of smoke from the hearth where we do our cooking. I can't help thinking what a long way I am from my cozy bedroom under the eaves.

October 20
Hunting

Mr. Audubon and I have gone hunting every day this week. We start out as soon as the sun is up. We leave the flatboat and arrange to meet it at an appointed place downstream. The first day we did this I couldn't believe that the boat wouldn't move faster than we did. But at dusk, when we came out of the woods, there it was.

We have found plenty of game as well as many birds to draw. Today, for example, we started out by taking care of our food supply. We shot seven partridges and a few grebes, which are a kind of duck. Later we came on a group of wild turkeys. Mr. Audubon showed me how he calls them. He has a whistle made of bone on which he blows. As soon as they hear the sound, they begin to flock around. He shot one, and it went into our gamebag with the other birds.

As for our drawing collection, I first shot a fish hawk, which I wounded. When I went to fetch it, the bird jabbed me in the hand with its talons. Then in its frantic twisting to get away it ran one of its claws through its own beak! Poor creature. Mr. Audubon killed it with a pin through the breast, so it would be whole for him to draw.

Soon after this, we added a hermit thrush to our collection.

When the gamebag became heavy, we decided to head back toward the river. That walk back to the boat seemed powerfully long to me, but Mr. A. stepped along as sprightly as if we were just starting out. By the time we saw the outlines of the boat looming out of the dusk, we had covered more than thirty miles. How does Mr. Audubon do it? He is almost forty years old, but I confess he can outlast me.

Right now he is sitting across from me in the cabin, setting up his drawing materials. He has everything the best— Whatman's paper, chalks, brushes, watercolor paints of the finest quality. When I marveled at his rich supplies, he told me, "Joseph, these are tools of my trade. For these and a good gun I will spend my last penny."

He lays out his supplies so lovingly—the way a man about to have a feast would set his table. How Mr. Audubon loves his work! He will labor all evening drawing the fish hawk and the hermit thrush. *He* is not a bit tired. But Joseph Mason is more than ready for sleep.

October 21
Working

Worked all day today. Practiced my flower drawing. Audubon is still drawing the fish hawk and the hermit thrush. He only made sketches of the hawk, but he has drawn the hermit thrush in detail and plans later to make a painting of it. Mr. A. makes sketches of everything as preparation for painting later. But if he makes a painting of a bird and later feels he can do it better, he will abandon or destroy the first one. At this rate I wonder, will he ever finish his portfolio?

It is very interesting how John James Audubon does his bird drawings, so I will tell it here. He has a wooden frame which is covered with wire. The wire is made of small squares. He wires the bird on this frame in some interesting and lifelike position. Sometimes he attaches threads to the wings and tail so he can raise or lower them. Then he takes fresh paper and rules it into squares the exact size of those on the frame. He then begins to draw the bird, true size, using the squares as a guide. He pays careful attention to every part, measuring bill and claw and length of wing. You might think all this measuring would make the drawing stiff and dull. But no. When Mr. Audubon is finished with the drawing, the bird looks so lively it seems that any moment it will fly off the paper.

After Mr. Audubon finished the drawing of the hermit thrush, he cut it open to examine the contents of its stomach. This way he can see what a bird has been eating and make note of it. Mr. A. makes a note of everything. He may someday write a book of life histories of the birds of America to go with his paintings.

I learned that we still weren't finished with the hermit

thrush. After he had finished examining it, Mr. A. put it into the fire and roasted it for our lunch! It was hardly enough for two, but what there was tasted tender and delicious. Still . . . I think I would rather hear a thrush sing than eat one. Mr. Audubon agreed.

October 28
In the Mud

Weather cold and colder. Glad to have those buffalo robes.

Yesterday we met a steamboat and tied up to it. It pulled us along at a good clip. Mr. Audubon says we are like baby ducklings paddling after our mama. Except that in this case we do no paddling; the wheel of the steamboat does the work. But it seems that nothing is gotten for nothing. Last night we paid dearly for our free ride. We had just curled up in our robes prepared to spend a quiet night when there was a terrible grinding sound. It threw everyone into an uproar, sent the hens skittering and clucking all over the deck. We had gone aground on a sandbar!

All the men had to turn out of bed to help get both boats unstuck. We climbed over the side and waded into the water, which was icy cold. The feeling left my legs altogether even though I was wearing my buckskins. Finally, after much pushing and shoving and a lot of cursing, we moved them both off the bar. Everyone clambered wearily back on deck and went into the cabin, where we hung our clothes in front of the fire and stationed ourselves there as well. We wrapped ourselves in the buffalo robes and waited for our breeches to dry; there was much chattering of teeth in the meantime.

Tired as I was, I remembered to remind Mr. Audubon that this dunking took care of my weekly bath. We bathe in the river on Sunday and wash our clothes. But I made him promise that I wouldn't have to face that cold water again for a full week!

November 10
Sickness

It has been a while since I last wrote. I have been sick, having suffered an accident. But let me tell it from the start.

It began with my wish to shoot a wild turkey. As I have mentioned, the woods here are filled with these handsome birds. And they make a fine dinner; the very thought of roasted turkey is enough to set my mouth to watering.

Everyone on the flatboat had managed to shoot a turkey. But the day that I got mine a poacher ran off with it. I had hung my gamebag on a tree while I was stalking, not knowing that the woods are full of thieving scoundrels. Came in for a lot of teasing on that account—"Ah, Joseph! Did you really shoot a bird or is it a tall tale?" Even Mr. Audubon, who saw me shoot the turkey, joined in the sport, for he is a great teaser. I was smarting from all of that and determined to get another bird.

Came a crisp morning, I set out. Mr. Audubon was busy painting, so I went with Captain Aumack. We had fine luck, and by the middle of the afternoon we had each bagged a pair of turkeys. As we approached the boat, I hallooed and held up my prizes for everyone to see. I was rewarded by cheers from the sailors on the deck. Then wasn't I proud!

But "Pride goeth before a fall," says the Good Book. As we waded toward the boat, another flock of turkeys came from the woods. The crew began shooting at them from the boats, and one of the birds fell into the water quite near me. Like a good bird dog,

I went to retrieve it from the water. Little did I know that the creature was only wounded. As I came on it, the turkey lunged at me and fetched me a good clap on the side of the head with its beak. Startled, I dropped my bag and tumbled backward into the shallows, where my head and a rock met with a hard how-dee-do.

The next thing I knew I was on the deck of the flatboat and some rummy-breath sailors were bending over me. Mr. A. was there, looking worried, and so was Mr. Aumack, his face lit up apple-scarlet.

I was spitting water like a well pump and feeling mighty dizzy. Nobody looked to be settling down to stay in one place, so I closed my eyes again. Didn't open them up until the following day. By this time I had a lump on my head the size of a potato, and pain to match.

It has taken several days for my noggin to heal. I never did find out what happened to my turkeys. Burns me to think that someone else ate them. But there are plenty more wild turkeys between here and New Orleans, and I vow that one will find its way into range of my gun before this trip is out.

Mr. Audubon was very kind to me when I was ill. Whenever I was awake, he was at my side, watching over me. Often he would play music for me. He is a fine musician on both the fiddle and the flute. It was most pleasant to lie in bed and have Mr. Audubon entertain me. But it must have been hard on him. Mr. A. is a great outdoorsman. It makes him seasick to be cooped up in the cabin when the boat is moving. Also the smoke from the poor cooking hearth bothers his eyes and makes it difficult for him to work. Gives him a headache, he says. Only he calls it a "haddack," in his French way.

My being sick has had one benefit. It has given me a chance to watch John James Audubon at work. I never did see a man work as *hard* as he does. I have watched him sometimes sixteen hours a day, bent over the little drawing table in the cabin. And this place so cramped he can't even stand up straight to stretch his legs!

When my head is better I hope to copy Mr. Audubon's ways and work harder at my own drawing.

I feel sorry for Mr. Audubon. I think it is a shame that he works so hard and makes such fine pictures, yet is so poor. Perhaps when these paintings are finished, he will get the fame he deserves.

Dog Day

I think Mr. A felt bad about my head. Yesterday he said to me, "Joseph, how would you like to have a dog to retrieve our game for us?"

I told him heartily that I would. I love dogs. Besides, after that knock on the head, I want no more part in fetching game. So Mr. Audubon said that when the flatboat passed the town of Henderson, Kentucky, I could go and fetch his bitch, Dash, which he had left there when he moved.

He told me that while I was ill, he bought us a skiff to make our bird hunting easier. I wonder where he got the money. No doubt some citizen of these parts now has a portrait of himself instead of a boat. That's Mr. Audubon's usual way.

So yesterday afternoon Captain Cummings (a passenger) and I took the skiff and rowed to the Kentucky shore, where we had no trouble finding the man who had Mr. Audubon's dog. I had wondered that Mr. Audubon didn't come with us. I found out why during the conversation between Mr. Cummings and Dash's keeper. I got the drift that Mr. Audubon is not too highly thought of in Henderson. He was in jail for debt in that town, where he lived for several years. The man certainly had some harsh words for John James Audubon. "Wastrel." "No-account." "Spendthrift." Seems Mr. Audubon had a store but didn't attend to it. The man told Mr. Cummings that once Mr. Audubon almost lost a packhorse load of supplies for the store because he went off into the woods chasing a bird and forgot all about it.

It made me squirm to hear that man come down so hard on Mr. A. I could hardly believe he was talking about the same man I know. My Mr. Audubon is decent and hard-working. No flies on him when it comes to working as an artist. Although I can see that he surely wasn't cut out to be a businessman.

I decided I didn't like that Henderson man much. But the dog was another story. Dash and I took to each other right away. She spent the time walking back to the skiff in licking my hands and jumping on me with friendliness.

By the time we had finished palavering in Henderson, night was on us. No sooner had we stepped into the skiff than the weather turned bad. The wind began to scream, and the sky turned black. It poured; we couldn't see a foot in front of the boat. All we could do was head for where the flatboat was. But each time we rowed a few feet the wind carried us back. I didn't feel nearly so safe with Captain Cummings as I would have if Mr. Audubon were there. Mr. Cummings is an engineer, not an outdoorsman like Mr. Audubon.

Night, black water, and screaming wind. There's a picture for you, and not one I want to see again. Especially since I have since heard of people getting lost and drowned in just such a storm on the Ohio. It was one in the morning when we finally saw the lights of the flatboat. Mr. Audubon was waiting for us. He kissed me on both cheeks, French style. I thought he was about to kiss the *dog*, he was so happy to see us!

Last night I was more than glad to get under my buffalo robe. And I minded not at all that I had a black-haired, four-footed companion to share it with me.

November 11
A Quarrel

Winter weather has really set in. Snow and sleet and so bitter that even Mr. A. doesn't feel up to hunting. So everyone is in bad humor and blames us that there is no fresh game to eat. I don't know which is louder, the growling of the crew or the grumbling of our bellies. Mr. Seeg, the so-called cook, doesn't do much of it. Each person slices his own bacon from the piece hanging on the wall and fries it in the fire. Some don't even bother to fry it but eat it cold. Mr. A. and I cook ours and dip the hard biscuits into the grease. It makes a tolerable meal, but we all think of roast turkey or partridge. The crew has a bit of whiskey on cold mornings, but Mr. A. drinks nothing but milk. He says he likes his shooting arm always to be steady. And he is a truly amazing shot. He can even bark a squirrel off a tree. This is a trick where you hit the bark just above the animal and it is knocked unconscious by the noise of the shot. Mr. A. says he learned this trick from Daniel Boone!

Last night all the bad feelings came out. It was partly my fault. After it was over, Mr. A. told me I had committed a *faux pas*, which is French for doing something wrong.

The evening started out jolly. We were all sitting around joking and telling stories. The cook had just brought out a piece of cheese for our supper. We were about to put our knives into it when we were startled to see something coming *out* of it. *Maggots*. Maggots are nasty, white, wormy things. Mr. A. says they are the infants of flies. Turned my stomach to see them, but the crew were already in their cups and thought it very funny. Mr. Audubon, always the scientist, was interested in how the maggots moved. He decided that they were flinging themselves about by folding their bodies in half and then snapping them full length again, thus moving themselves forward. He measured some of their "jumps" and said they were able to move forty or fifty times their length.

Seeing the maggots move made everyone even more merry. Each man chose a maggot and began to lay bets on which one would get the farthest. In the midst of this friendly game Mr. Seeg turned mean. Where, he demanded, was Mr. Audubon going to get the money to pay up if he should lose the bet? Everyone knew, he said sneeringly, that Mr. Audubon was a pauper and owed money to everyone in Kentucky and a few in Pennsylvania besides.

Mr. Audubon turned very white and quiet. I felt so sorry for him because I knew at once what had happened. Mr. Cummings had spread the stories he heard from the man in Henderson.

I guess I lost my head. I flew at Seeg. "Don't you dare talk about Mr. Audubon that way," I said. "He is a great man and a great painter, and someday he will be famous." In my rage I pounded on his chest. The cook grabbed me by the neck and began to cuff me. Then he picked up his meat knife and came for me.

Mr. Audubon moved so quickly no one even saw him get up. Before anyone knew what had happened, he had Seeg's arm pinned behind his back and had forced the knife out of his hand. Mr. Seeg staggered backward and would have fallen if someone hadn't caught him. Everyone started to laugh, and that should have been the end of it. But Seeg wanted to show he was peeved, so he walked out of the cabin. He was so drunk he forgot where he was. When we heard a splash and ran out on deck we discovered that he had walked right off the boat into the water!

I believe those ruffians would have let him drown. But Mr. A. quickly got one of the poling oars and handed it out to him. By that device the cook was able to pole himself to shore. He stumbled away, into the darkness.

That was the last we saw of him. So now the boat is short-handed by one man, and we are without a cook. Captain Aumack says that since I was the cause of the trouble, I must be the cook. Beggars can't be choosers, I guess. Mr. Audubon chuckles about my new role, but I don't think it's funny. The more chores I have, the less time I can spend on my drawing. And I am getting a powerful hankering to spend more time at it, thanks to John James Audubon!

October 20
Mr. Audubon's Story

We thought that Dash had forgotten how to hunt, and Mr. Audubon called her "good-for-nothing." But now we know the reason for her slowness. Our Dash will shortly become a mother!

Today it rained so hard that we were forced to stay in the

cabin. After we drew for a while and Mr. A. showed me some tricks with color and shading, we sat and talked. Mr. Audubon told me some things about his life that he has told no one else. I'm glad he chose me to tell his tale to; Mr. Audubon is a born storyteller. Listening to him is better than reading from the most exciting book.

John James Audubon was born on the island of Santo Domingo. His father, who was a French sea captain, had a plantation there. His mother died very soon after he was born. I think from what he *doesn't* say that Mr. Audubon's mother and father weren't married. When he was three he went to France, where his father's wife took him for her son and raised him with love and devotion.

I think that Mr. Audubon was rich when he was young. He tells me of parties and servants and a house in the country, where he first became interested in birds. He said he used to sneak off into the woods to watch birds when he should have been in school. He had a fine collection of birds' nests and eggs by the time he was ten years old.

One thing that happened when he was a little boy seems to have had a deep effect on him. There was a pet monkey in his house. Also a beautiful parrot. One day the monkey killed the bird in a fit of jealousy. Mr. Audubon never forgot it; he was heartbroken for the bird.

"But you kill birds all the time," I said to him. "If you love them so much, why do you kill them?"

"What I kill I use for my work or to feed us," he said. "If I could draw my birds without killing them, I surely would."

He grew sad. I hoped I hadn't put him in that mood. But I have seen him that way before. One minute he can be laughing and happy as a lark. The next moment he is plunged into the deepest gloom or complaining of headache and sea sickness (which he calls *mal de mer*).

I begged his pardon for making him sad. He said I hadn't done it. He said he had been looking at his wife's picture, and it seemed to him that her eyes looked strange. He feels there is something wrong at home and the picture is an omen of it. Mr. Audubon surely is a queer fish. But his worry has set me thinking. Neither one of us has gotten any mail from home since we left. There is no way to get mail except when we stop a steamboat and exchange packets. So far there has been nothing for us. Mr. Audubon's gloom has now fastened on me. I feel as sad as my teacher. I did not bargain for lessons in sadness!

Tonight Mr. Audubon finished the story of his life. He went from rich to poor soon after he came to America, and he is still in that latter condition. If it were not for his wife, he admits, his children would often not have enough to eat. Lucy Audubon works as a governess and supports the family. But still Mr. Audubon is determined to do his book. I hope in my heart he will, for I believe him to be a great man who only lacks for recognition.

The Eagles' Day

We have left the Ohio River and are now on the broad, muddy waters of the Mississippi. A few days ago, when we got to the place where they come together, Mr. Audubon said it reminded him of the young person who comes "from the pure stream of youth and is swallowed up by the turbulent waters of life." He was in one of his gloomy moods again.

But today he seemed happy. He even played his flute a bit as we drifted along. I say drifted because we have a new way to go. Instead of walking, we launch the skiff and float ahead of the flatboat. It is usually the three of us, Mr. Audubon, Dash, and I. We stay low, like Indians. When we see game Mr. A. and I sit up, aim our guns, and shoot.

When we started, the weather was gray and cloudy. There was a light frost, and the animals were on the move to warmer weather. We watched huge flocks of geese and ducks passing overhead all morning. Mr. Audubon noted which direction they were going and what species they were.

We were out about an hour when the clouds lifted and the sun began to shine. The sun on my back was a good feeling. Even Dash seemed to enjoy it and lay quietly in the boat, basking. She is quite agile, considering that she will have her pups in about a week.

All nature seemed to be working with us today. Or maybe Mr. Audubon is the Pied Piper with that flute of his. At any rate, we saw all sorts of wildlife. Bear, deer, beaver, otter—all manner of creatures were out today.

Passed a lot of sandbars and little spits of willow-covered land. These are called towheads. When the water is high, they become islands or else are completely covered.

The woods on both banks of the river are filled with wildfowl. Every tree has its tenants. We are looking hard to find new species, as well as other examples of the birds Mr. Audubon is already working on. I'm beginning to see what a tremendous job he has set for himself. He can't even rely on one example of each bird. He has to get both male and female, note if their coloring differs at different times of the year, and make sure that a bird is truly a new species and not merely the young of a species he has already painted.

It's a weighty matter. And the penalty for being wrong is to have other scientists laugh at you. Mr. Audubon is very much afraid of that. He says that some people hold it against him that he is not a trained scientist. Trained indeed! It seems to me John James Audubon knows more about the habits of birds than any man living.

But to get back to our outing. . . . We shot a number of birds, including one enormous turkey cock, which we planned to use for dinner. I didn't relish the thought of plucking that bird, although I knew the job would fall to me since I am still official cook.

It was when we were drifting around a bend in the river that we saw the eagles. A female was on a high limb of a tree and was being approached by a male. She squatted when she saw him coming, and he landed on top of her. They mated, to the accompaniment of a lot of cackling. It was over shortly, and the male sailed off, with the female right behind him. We watched them dancing in the air together for some time.

Mr. Audubon made notes about it, "December—yet the eagles are mating and nesting here," he wrote, along with a description much like what I've told here.

I asked Mr. A. why he didn't shoot at them. I know he is anxious to have the white-headed eagle among his drawings. He smiled and looked a little sheepish and said he would not interrupt them in their lovemaking!

A little while later we passed under an eagle's nest on the branches of a cypress tree. It was an enormous construction— not less than eight feet across. There were several eagles flying about. There was no way to tell which one the nest belonged to.

Now we began to see eagles all around. They were sitting in the low branches of trees along the river. They did not move as we drifted by in our little boat. I decided that they were making us a gift of their presence since we hadn't killed their fellows. It wasn't a very scientific idea, but it pleased me.

We continued to drift. We didn't even fire our guns at other birds for fear of disturbing the eagles. Mr. Audubon said this was to be his day for observing them. We noticed that some eagles have brown heads. Others are white on top. Mr. Audubon's notion is that they are two different species. He looked at them all carefully through his spyglass and let me try it once or twice. Truly, that is a wonderful tool. It makes everything you look at seem close at hand.

We had put out a fishing line as we were drifting, hoping to catch something. In the late afternoon we felt a tremendous tug on the line. After much sweat and muscle, we finally hauled aboard a monster catfish. I think it must have been close to sixty pounds—truly a magnificent fish. We stared at it as it slapped about in the bottom of the skiff. Suddenly Audubon said, "Ah! Yes! I have it! I will draw my eagle with the catfish. I will put the fish in the eagle's talons." As soon as he said it, I realized what a good idea it was. Most of the bird paintings I have seen show the creature simply sitting on a branch. But Mr. Audubon is talking about painting *scenes* of birds doing what they do in the wild.

Sitting there in the boat, he made his first sketches, just as he saw it in his imagination. But he was handicapped without an eagle to draw from. It was then that we decided to try to bring one down without killing it. We both tried, but I am no match for John Audubon in shooting skill. He finally pointed out an eagle, told me which wing he was going to hit, and proceeded to do it, from *150 yards away!*

The eagle fell, wounded. In spite of her swollen belly, faithful Dash plunged into the water and started after it. We followed in the skiff and succeeded in hauling both dog and eagle back into the boat. The eagle, safely captured, sat glaring at us, while his mate circled our boat shrieking with rage and sorrow, in a most pitiable way.

When we arrived back at the boat, we showed everyone our prize. Then we fastened him to a perch. But we neglected to fasten the perch securely, and the next thing we knew, friend eagle had departed, dragging the long pole behind him. He skimmed across the water, half fluttering, half swimming. I had to go out after him again in the small boat, and once again make him captive.

What a magnificent, brave bird. He sits on his perch and glares at the world. When anyone comes near, he ruffles up his feathers like an owl. Tonight we cut up the catfish and fed him some, offering it to him at the end of the stick. Once, when Mr. Audubon was leaning forward to feed him, he suddenly shot out a talon and caught Mr. A. a nasty blow on his right thumb. I hope it won't interfere with his drawing. A drawing of the eagle should be splendid.

Speaking of drawing, I keep asking Mr. Audubon when I will be ready to do some work on his paintings, like a real apprentice. Why won't he let me paint in a background or draw the feet of a bird? I'm sure I could do some of the flower background well.

"Not yet, Joseph," he tells me. "You must do a bit more work with the pen. More accurate. More rhythm. You must *look* more and get your hand to do the bidding of your eye." Dear heaven, what a taskmaster John James Audubon is.

Today I made a birthing bed for Dash, who is ready to whelp any day.

Saw some amazing plants, including my first glimpse of Spanish beard hanging on the trees. I hear this moss lives on air and needs no soil to grow in. Also saw a plant in full bloom (in December!). Sometimes I think that if I knew plants well enough, I would not need a map or calendar but could tell just where I was and what time of year by the green things about me.

December 25
Christmas

Today started badly. Both of us were feeling low to be so far from home on Christmas Day. All Christmas means on a flatboat is that everyone drinks a little more than usual, or, as Mr. A. says, they put more *spirits* than *spirit* into the occasion.

In the morning Mr. Audubon and I exchanged gifts. He gave me a portrait he had done of me, which I shall treasure. I gave him a drawing I had made of some flowering plants, which seemed to please him mightily.

The boat got stuck again this morning. One of the crew broke the poling oars, so we all had to go on shore and pull the boat along with a towrope. Truly, these boats are good for nothing. They cannot go at all unless someone pushes, pulls, tows, tugs. . . . Last week we were so mired in mud we had to go ashore and find a farmer with a team of horses to get us out of our mess. Now I ask you, what kind of boat is that? And what kind of boat is it that can only go one way—downstream? The flatboat will be useless once it gets to New Orleans. There it will be broken up and the lumber sold. Or else it will be left to rot on shore. And a fitting fate for it, too, if you ask me. I can't wait to get off and will gladly help take an ax to it. Last evening the wind blew so hard through the slits in the wall that I shook with cold, and all the drawings I did are full of wiggly lines.

Celebrated the holiday by taking a tramp through the woods and a row down the Yazoo River. The weather is like May, warm and pleasant. Saw *millions* of cormorants flying south. "The dung is falling like snowflakes," Mr. Audubon said.

Came on two canoes full of Indians, which tickled Mr. A. He likes nothing better than to palaver with the Indians, whom he admires greatly. These were of the Osage tribe and very friendly. We tried to talk, but they didn't understand English or French. So Mr. A. hit on the idea of talking to them with pictures. I reckon one picture is worth a barrel of words because we all got on famously after that. When we got hungry, Mr. Audubon drew a picture of a deer with a stroke across the hind parts, to show them that we would like some venison hams. They disappeared and came back with two handsome legs of venison. Mr. Audubon paid the Indians fifty cents and gave them a couple of loads of gunpowder, and they went away happy.

We built our fire near the shore in a sheltered cove. When it was high and hot, we threw on some sweet potatoes, which we'd brought with us. Then I skewered some strips of venison and roasted them over the fire. When they were crisp and black outside and juicy and tender inside, we ate them. That, along with our hot sweet potatoes, was our Christmas dinner, and a fine one it was, too.

We had just about swallowed the last bite when we heard shouts from the flatboat. We jumped into our skiff and rowed to within calling distance, where we learned that Dash was about to have her litter. I rowed like a demon; didn't want to miss that event.

We arrived at the boat just as the first pup was being born. The tiny creature presented itself in a sac, which Dash tore open with her teeth. Then she licked the pup clean and bit the cord that attached it to her. She did this ten times. All the pups were born alive and well.

Soon after they were born, Mr. Audubon did something strange. I still do not understand it completely but will give an account of it here.

As we sat watching Dash nurse her pups, Mr. Audubon said, "She will be wanting food after her labors." He got up himself and began making something over the fire. In a while he was back with some sort of boiled mess. I asked him what it was.

"Parakeet hearts," he said. I remembered then that we had killed several Carolina parakeets the day before.

"Why just the hearts?" I asked, thinking it was a perhaps some special medicine for dogs who have just given birth.

"It's an experiment," says he. "The hearts of parakeets are supposed to be poisonous to a dog. But I am sure that it is an old wives' tale," he added. "I want to test if I am right."

I could not believe my ears.

"But what if you are wrong?" I asked.

"Then we will have learned something."

"But your own dog," I sputtered. "Dash, whom you know and love. . . ."

"What then? Would you have me do it to another man's dog?" he asked me.

"Don't do it at all," I begged. I went to take the dish away from Dash, but she was already at it.

The next hours were torture. But Mr. Audubon worked at his drawing board as if nothing was happening.

Two hours later Dash was back nursing her pups. She never showed any ill effects from what Mr. A. afterward referred to as

31

her "heart-y" meal. But I was sick at my stomach from the thought of what could have happened.

I guess Mr. A. must have been pretty sure nothing would happen, or he wouldn't have taken the risk. Still . . . he is a most puzzling person in many ways. Did I tell here about the night that he dressed up in a French sailor's costume? Oh—he looked fine, with earrings dangling and a bandanna wrapped around his head. Danced and sang us French songs all evening as merry as a cricket. The next day no one could get a word from him. All the gaiety was gone.

I don't think I understand John James Audubon at all.

December 27
Natchez

Yesterday morning we floated into the harbor at Natchez. I couldn't wait to get off the boat, but my "master" told me I must stay and watch our gear. So he left me and went off with Mr. Berthoud, who is a relative of his. He came back this morning washed and well fed and looking as if he had had a fine night's sleep under clean sheets. Not a word that I had been left to fend for myself and to take care of Dash. He had simply forgotten all about me.

How I hate this boat life! Let other boys stow away on boats. I am thinking to sneak off this tub and stow away on shore!

I am sick of Mr. John James Audubon, too, if the truth be known. All he cares about are *his* precious *birds* and *his* painting. He thinks more of his gun than he does of any person, excepting maybe members of his family. Even there he has a funny way of showing his affection. He's away from them more often than not. Anyway, I'm plumb tired of him and of his moods, too. Never know if he'll be cheerful or glum. Never praises me for my work, which I *know* is getting better all the time. Maybe he's jealous. Wouldn't put *that* past him. He has a fine opinion of himself. Thinks he's the world's greatest artist.

Ah, this place. It's making me low in my mind and turning my stomach. The cabin always and forever smells of dead birds. By the time the *great artist* is finished with them they have set up such a stink in here one can scarcely stand it. And it brings the rats, too. Yesterday, a rat ran off with a vireo skin before Mr. Audubon could even draw it.

I am a rugged boy, I think, and well used to a rough life. But I tell you I am sick to death of this flatboat.

Nor have I heard from my family. That does not help my mood. Only one letter this whole time. I hope, please God, they are weathering the winter well and my father's health is better.

We will all go to bed now. By "we" I mean myself and the various biting, stinging, crawling creatures that seem to have made a home in my buffalo robe.

Part Two
New Orleans

January 1, 1821
New Year

Well. This new year is starting better than the old one
ended. We've left the flatboat and are sailing toward New
Orleans on a keelboat owned by Mr. Audubon's relative, Mr.
Berthoud. It must be a favor that we're here, because Mr.
Audubon surely can't pay for our passage. He must be the poor-
est man aboard. We didn't even have a whole pair of boots
between us until Mr. Audubon went ashore and found a shoe-
maker who was willing to give us new footwear in
exchange for a portrait of himself.

No matter. We are here and both feeling cheerful again. Had
a proper bath and washed and dried our clothes. Cut each
other's hair, so now although our locks are still long, we do not

look *quite* so hairy. I do believe I am getting whiskers. Maybe I shall come home with a beard, like my good teacher.

Mr. Berthoud is traveling on the keelboat, too. He has given us the use of his servants. Joy! *No more cooking for me!* How pleasant it is to sit down at a meal that someone else has prepared. Something funny—supper tonight being our first meal in a long time at a respectable table, both Mr. Audubon and I picked up our food with our fingers. The looks we got from the others soon reminded us that we were back among refined folks—where they have other tools than fingers for eating!

Is it possible that Mr. Audubon and I have grown too used to our frontier life? We both felt awkward at the table and found the conversation boring. One man spent the whole meal talking about a new *corset* he had ordered from England. I think I prefer the rummy sailors of the flatboat to these silk-shirted fops.

But the keelboat itself is in every way superior to the flatboat. The cabin is larger and more comfortable, and the keelboat has a pointed front, which can cut through the water speedily. It also has sails, as well as eight rowers, in case the wind should fail. Right now we are tied behind a steamboat, so we are moving along smartly.

It seems to me that I can already feel the softness of the southern breezes. Yes, Joseph Mason is happy tonight.

The Portfolio

A new crisis. Mr. Audubon's portfolio is missing. It must have been left on the dock at Natchez when we changed boats. I'm glad *I* didn't have anything to do with that. It was Mr. Berthoud's servant who left it.

Mr. Audubon is like a crazy man. He paces up and down the deck, wringing his hands and talking to himself in French. He told me he has visions of some "ruffian" taking his beautiful bird drawings and using them to wrap an oar or pinning them up in the cabin of a flatboat!

Truly, it is a shame. All that work. I know for a fact the eagle drawing alone took him sixty hours. And we count there are about fifteen or sixteen other drawings that are missing. Luckily, Mr. Audubon has left most of his earlier work at home with Mrs. A. Still, it's very discouraging to have your *latest* work lost. Mr. Audubon feels that these paintings were full of his newest and best ideas.

What's to be done now? Mr. A. has sent messages to friends in Natchez asking them to inquire about the portfolio at the dock and also to put an advertisement in the newspaper. I do hope it's found.

I carried my portfolio onto the keelboat myself. It now contains about a hundred sketches of plants and flowers, as well as drawings of birds, insects, frogs—anything that we captured or plucked. I like leafing through them and seeing my progress, for progress it certainly is.

The Swamp

We left the steamboat (or rather it left us), and we have been sailing for three days. We're beginning to pass large plantations and fields of cotton and sugar cane. These plantation houses are different from our plain wood and brick houses back in Ohio. Much ironwork in the Spanish style and very elegant.

Today and yesterday we left the boat and went walking into the bayous that line the shore. Strange world—cypress trees and Spanish beard, ferns and a plant called the palmetto, which is new to me. How I love plants, especially the plants and trees of a swamp! People don't look nearly enough at plants; otherwise they would see the great variety in colors and shapes. My favorites are the tiny plants that float on the water and form a green carpet through which the frogs and turtles poke their heads. I don't know their name—I have never been in a swamp before.

Some of the water is brown with the stain of cedar. It is so clear in places you can see the bottom. Some plants grow large leaves and seem to live completely on trees. I wonder do they get their nourishment from their hosts?

There are mockingbirds everywhere. Of all the birds in the woods, I think I like the mockingbirds best. We even hear them at night. And how they can imitate the call of other birds! Many times we chase a new sound only to find that it is our friend mockingbird, teasing us. Mockingbirds will imitate anything. Mr. Audubon says he once heard one imitate the town crier calling "All's well" in the evening.

Today I shot and killed two warblers. When we came home, Mr. A. laid them out and sketched them by candlelight; he wanted to get a good start painting in the morning.

Mr. Audubon is busy these days working on a portrait of Mr. Eickerson, the master of this boat. Mr. Eickerson is paying in gold, which is good. We need the money badly. Whenever Mr. A. gets a few dollars together, he sends them home to his family. So we are always short of cash for our own needs and always scrounging.

Today Mr. Audubon shot some terns and a winter falcon. As

we were walking back toward our skiff, we passed some slaves cutting sugar cane. They begged us to give them the falcon, saying that it would be a great treat for them to eat. They seemed so wretched Mr. Audubon gave it to them. Seems a hard lot to be a slave.

When we got back to the keelboat, both Mr. Audubon and I sketched the terns. He was much pleased with what I did and told me so. Said that my sketch had spirit and excellent proportion. That sends me to bed tonight in a fine humor. It's rare that I get a compliment from the great John James Audubon!

We are approaching New Orleans. Mr. Audubon says I may have a whole day there to myself.

New Orleans

I have had my day—and quite an adventure it was. We arrived at the dock about eight this morning. We were greeted by the sight of hundreds of fish crows wheeling over our heads. Like gulls, the fish crows hang about the wharves, picking up garbage tossed off the boats.

The dock is enormously busy, and so is the town around it. It is crowded with people of every color—Negroes, Creoles, turbaned mulatto women, a great many Indians in colorful blankets, and some gentlemen in fancy clothes. They must be from Europe or from the plantations we saw along the way. Everyone was talking at once, having a fine time bargaining.

People bargain here for everything. The marketplace in New Orleans must be the most unusual one in the world for variety of products. One thing that they have aplenty is what we are always looking for—birds. I have never seen so many kinds of birds in my life. New Orleans people must eat everything in the way of birds. I even saw a barred owl for sale—twenty-five cents. Barred owl for dinner? I've eaten a mess of different birds since I came on this trip, but barred owl, roasted, boiled, stew or fried, is a new idea to me. Back home in Ohio we have owls in our barns, not in our cooking pots!

I went to find Mr. Audubon, sure that my friend would want to share the sights with me. Found him in Mr. Berthoud's office, yawning from the company of a group of businessmen and happy to get away.

We went back to the market together and walked smack into the middle of a parade and celebration of the Battle of New Orleans. It was a noisy affair and didn't seem to do much to cheer Mr. Audubon, who is missing his family again and glum because today is a holiday and he cannot look for mail. The parade was of little interest to us. We saw the governor and a lot of strutting soldiers. I would rather have been in the woods seeing a row of jack-in-the-pulpits. As for Mr. A., the day was a disaster. When the parade was over, Mr. A. reached into his trousers only to discover that his pocketbook was missing. A pickpocket must have made off with it. As usual, there was no money in it, but there was a fortune in letters from important people, which Mr. Audubon could have used to get work. Now they are gone, like the portfolio.

It sometimes seems that everything conspires to keep Mr. Audubon from succeeding in his career. Tonight at supper he told me a list of the discouragements he has suffered. One time he left 200 drawings in a friend's attic. When he came to claim them some months later, he discovered that rats had chewed them to bits. Another time Mr. A. lost all his money on a poor business venture in a mill. He has been in jail and in debt and was once stabbed by a man.

I keep changing my feeling about Mr. Audubon. Sometimes I almost hate him. Other times I feel so sorry for him. But one thing is always the same—my admiration for his work. He is a great artist, of that I am sure.

New Orleans, we've decided, is the dirtiest city in the world. "When you are poor," says Mr. Audubon, "you feel it most when you are in a city." By this I think he means that there are always things to buy in a city. Mr. A. loves nice things. He saw a set of china in a shop the other day . . . he wanted so much to buy it for Mrs. Audubon. . . . Last night he wanted to go to the quadroon's ball, which is a lively occasion here. But it costs a dollar. So he didn't go but stood outside listening to the music, like a hungry boy in front of the pastry shop.

Mail

Mail today! I was glad to hear from my parents, but I sense that there's something they're not telling me in their letters. Mr. Audubon didn't seem so glad to hear from his family. Walked around with a face down to his knees all day after getting that letter from Mrs. A. I think he has asked her to come here and join him and she has refused. She probably wanted to know if he is making enough money to support the family if she gives up her job. The answer to that is no. I wish I could help Mr. A. make money. Paint portraits. Something. Right now we eat from our hunting and sleep on the boat. But when the boat leaves, what shall we do? Mr. Audubon is trying mightily to get work. He shows his birds, and everyone admires them, but no one gives him work. "We can't live on compliments," he says bitterly. It galls him that artists not as skillful as he are busy painting portraits in this town.

Sometimes I think I won't be an artist when I grow up. It's too hard to make a living from it.

I go down to the docks every morning to greet the boats

coming down from Natchez and to inquire about the lost portfolio. So far no luck.

Painting Portraits

Things are much better than they were last time I wrote here. Mr. Audubon has got himself several jobs painting portraits. (Maybe he should switch from birds to *people*. At least people pay to have their portraits painted.)

One of Mr. Audubon's jobs has been drawing death masks. When someone dies, they call Mr. Audubon in to make a last portrait of the dying or dead person for the family. Sometimes he gets called out in the middle of the night. Now here's a gruesome story. A parson here in New Orleans saw Mr. Audubon's work and liked it. The man had a son who had just died. Well, would you believe the minister dug up the body of his child so Mr. Audubon could draw it! Was very pleased with the results, too.

What a strange business it is to be an artist. Something like being a magician, I reckon. Take a piece of paper and some colors, and make something dead seem alive.

No matter how busy Mr. Audubon is with his portraits, he manages to do some work on his birds every day. We are better situated for him to work now. We are off the boat and living in a rented room in New Orleans. Our room, for which we pay ten dollars a month, has a grocery store on either side. This provides us with some entertainment, for the walls are so thin that we get a fair amount of the gossip of New Orleans without moving from our room.

In spite of this "attraction," we spend very little time there. After my drawing hours, I go hunting or exploring in the woods. Mr. A. is generally occupied with his portraits. If not, he comes with me and then does his bird painting at night.

New Orleans is an odd place. Can't seem to make up its mind whether to be land or water. After a heavy rain the river rises and floods the streets. The people seem used to it. They stand on their balconies or galleries, as they call them, and watch the Mississippi wash past their doorsteps.

Yesterday we went for a walk in the woods (more like a wade in the woods, it's so swampy). The plants are something quite marvelous, as I've said here before. And to see them in bloom in February! It made me itch for my drawing pencil, I tell you. Took some specimens back to the room wrapped in damp moss and looked up the names in Mr. Audubon's copy of *Linnaeus.*

You can't learn *anything* about nature by asking these people around here. We asked someone where he got a certain bird. When he shrugged and said he couldn't remember, Mr. Audubon muttered that he was a stupid ass. There are funny local names for everything. For example, the bird we call a snipe they call *cache cache.* What we call a godwit is here called *clou clou.* And with the plants it is likewise.

Mr. Audubon has sent some new paintings back to Mrs. Audubon on Mr. Berthoud's keelboat. The amount of work he does is extraordinary, for in the past six months he has completed twenty paintings and hundreds of sketches and drawings.

Still the portfolio hasn't turned up.

42

Bird Life

We have been watching the migration of birds. This is a subject in which Mr. Audubon is very interested. To tell the truth, until I met John James Audubon, I didn't even know that birds travel from one part of the country to another. When I was small, I was told that I didn't see certain birds in winter because they were sleeping under the mud or even under the water! There are plenty of folks who still believe this way, although Mr. Audubon says it is absolutely not true.

He says that birds migrate to warmer climates to get food. Sometimes they travel hundreds of miles without stopping to get their winter homes. But I asked Mr. Audubon, "How do they know where to go and how to get there? And do they go to the same place every year?"

He admits that is a puzzle. But someday, he says, scientists will have a system for marking birds and following their movements. He says he once marked a phoebe by tying a string on its leg. Through this device he discovered that the phoebe came back to the same nest the following year.

Today we saw some migrating birds and also a terrible slaughter of them. We were walking along the shore of a lake when we spied a huge flock of golden plovers. There were thousands of them, coming from the northeast and heading south. Ordinarily, Mr. Audubon says, these birds fly over water, but a storm at sea had blown them in toward land.

The hunters, knowing their ways, were waiting for them, stationed all around the woods. They began to use their bird-calls, which imitate the call of the golden plover. The poor birds heard that *Qu-ee-a! Qu-ee-a!* and turned toward the sound. They came directly overhead. As they wheeled, every man raised his gun. At the first volley, hundreds of birds fell.

The sound of firing kept up all day; when we were going home, they were still at it. We stopped to talk to them at sunset.

One man told us he had shot 750 birds! There were about 400 gunners out there today. According to my sums, if each of them brought down close to what that hunter did, the day's shooting could have accounted for over a quarter of a *million* birds.

Mr. Audubon says he has seen the same massacre of the passenger pigeon. We have decided, Mr. Audubon and I, that while we like hunting as much as the next fellow, this kind of wholesale butchery makes us sick.

"Don't you notice fewer and fewer birds each year?" Mr. Audubon asked the hunters. They said no. Probably what saves the plovers is that they only come this far into shore during a storm. I wish I could tell them, "Brave the storm rather than risk the hunters."

March 5
Found

A lucky day for us. The portfolio has been found! It is at the newspaper office in Natchez. And from what we understand, only one drawing is missing. Mr. A. picked up his fiddle when he heard the news and has been playing and singing, perky as a catbird ever since. I am so happy for him.

Lately, I am devoting myself to two jobs—my drawing and finding birds for Mr. Audubon. We both draw every day, Sundays, too. My teacher pointed out to me that if I skip one day, the hand loses some skill and it takes two days to make it up.

Sunday is my favorite day here. On Sunday we have a quiet morning. We write letters. Mr. A. spends a lot of time looking at his wife's picture and sighing. After this "meditating" time we bathe and wash our clothes or give them to the landlady to wash. Then, after eating our lunch, we get out our drawing pencils and work all afternoon.

If Mr. Audubon has had a good week, we have our dinner at an inn, where we sample the good shrimps and other seafood of these parts. How I love this. Afterward we go to the Museum Coffee Shop, where we sit and talk with other artists and play cards or watch the roulette games and listen to music.

Even in a bad week, we manage to eat well. We are both good shots, and game is plentiful around here. A good thing, for Mr. Audubon will never eat a piece of meat from a butcher shop or a market. "Only fresh game, fresh fish, and fresh vegetables," he says. Says he learned that from an Indian philosopher. What an odd man he is. Did I mention in these pages that John James Audubon takes snuff? Now there's something I don't think I have a hankering for. Seems to me there's not much to taking a pinch of that powder and sticking it up your nose and then giving a sneeze or two. Mr. A. admits it's a silly habit and is always saying he's going to quit it, but I wouldn't put a wager on it.

Quicksand

Don't think we are neglecting our nature searches in favor of city life. But after I tell yesterday's adventure, you may think

I would have been better off staying in front of the Museum Coffee Shop, listening to Mr. A. play his flute.

There is a sandy bottom lake that we can walk to from our house. We decided to go there in search of birds. It was barely day when we left. The mists still hung over the water, and that, with the Spanish moss, gave a ghostly character to the land. I followed Mr. Audubon through the canebrake, listening for bird sounds and trying to avoid snakes. When the sun rose and burned off the mists, we were able to see who was up and about. Now we observed frogs, aswell as turtles of several species lying on logs or branches in the water. Innumerable small lizards ran up and down the cypress trees. We noticed that the Mississippi kites were feeding on them.

"There's an idea for a painting," I said to Mr. Audubon. And he agreed.

I spied an alligator lying like a log on the bank. It looked so still I was sure it was dead. Mr. Audubon said not to be fooled and told me that one alligator had eaten a man's hunting dog. He advised me always to look sharp before I step on any logs along the shore!

Soon we decided to separate, so that we could cover more territory in our search for birds. It was our plan to meet back at the spot in an hour.

Not long after we parted company, I heard a faint whirring of wings. Looking up, I spied a barred owl. I decided to follow it, hoping that it would find a spot, light there and sit quietly, as owls usually do during the day. I hoped to get the owl for Mr. Audubon, who does not yet have a painting of this bird. So, head up to watch my quarry, I plunged through the swamp. I forgot about snakes, alligators, everything. I was watching the owl.

Quiet. Only the sucking sound of my boots going through the muck. At last—I saw the owl through the trees. It was sitting motionless, its head turned away from me. If I hadn't been on the lookout for it, I would have mistaken it for a clump of moss or some dead leaves.

I raised my gun ever so quietly. Then, thinking to get an even closer shot at it, I began to move forward. I took one step, then another, then. . . .

Before I knew what was happening, I began to sink. The most terrible feeling of my life passed over me. I was in quicksand!

I had the presence of mind to toss my gun away, so my hands would be free. I grappled with the twisted roots around me, trying to get a grip somewhere. But it was no use. When the horrid ooze was about up to my armpits, I started to yell. I was surprised to hear the pure terror in my scream for help. But I knew that if Mr. Audubon wasn't around, Joseph Mason wasn't going to be around much longer either.

How fine the sound of someone crashing through the woods can be! In a few minutes, Mr. Audubon appeared. He took one look at my situation and knew what to do. He found a stout branch and pushed it out to me. I grabbed it, and by this means he pulled me to firm ground.

"Well, Joseph," says he. "What were you after that made you forget to look where you were going?" I told him about the owl, and nothing would do but we must try to find it again, in spite of the fact that I was covered with mud and more than ready to quit for the day. John James Audubon can be the most persistent man! But I knew that it would have been no different if *he* had been the one to fall in the quicksand. So we continued our search for the owl, and I suffered my muddy clothes in silence.

An hour later we came on the owl again. It was about to swoop down on a squirrel. Mr. A. took aim and brought it down with one shot. As we walked home with our prize, Mr. Audubon said he wanted to draw it just as he found it.

And that is the way he has started it, with the squirrel in the picture, too.

All the practice has not been wasted. Today at last I did my first professional drawing.

We had gone out early in search of plants to put in Mr. Audubon's drawings. Found some jewelweed and a pink orchid. And not only did we find several plants in bloom, but I shot what must be the loveliest little bird in the world. It is called the yellow-backed blue warbler. First I found the male and then the female. They are both a wonderful shade of blue and yellow.

Mr. Audubon was very excited. We came straight home, where he began to work on them immediately. About five in the afternoon Mr. A. called me over to see his work. I was astonished to see that he had drawn the birds on a drawing of an iris that I made the previous day.

I can't tell how proud it has made me to see our work together. There are John James Audubon's beautiful birds, sitting on *my* iris. And down in the corner of the drawing Mr. Audubon has written, " *'Yellow-backed Blue Warbler,' by John James Audubon. Plants by Joseph Mason.*"

May 16, 1821

This day has brought me sad news. My father is dead. I can hardly write of it. All this time, these many weeks, my father has been dead, and I never knew it. How is it that I didn't sense somehow that he was gone?

Mr. Audubon is being kind. This evening we sat outside in the street in front of our house, talking quietly. We talked about our fathers. Mr. Audubon's father encouraged him to draw and paint, just as my father did with me.

"Papa brought me my first book of bird paintings," Mr. Audubon said. He wept and didn't seem ashamed of it. And that made it easier for me to let the tears fall.

Then Mr. A. went in and got his flute and played for a while. He never left my side the whole day. Now he is asleep, but sleep won't come to me. I can't believe I will never see my father again. . . .

Part Three
On Oakley

On the Water Again

Trying to forget the past and do my job here. It's easier now that we've left New Orleans, which is full of bad memories for me. We are on a steamboat going to southern Louisiana. There a family named Pirrie has promised to give us room and board on their plantation and sixty dollars a month in exchange for Mr. Audubon tutoring their daughter. Mr. A. is not particularly happy about this new job because he feels it may interfere with his bird work. But truly we have been leading a hand-to-mouth existence, so it's good that he has found something steady.

I am looking forward to living on a plantation. I hear that this one, *Oakley,* is very beautiful. Mr. Audubon should be happy to be getting off the boat. He has been seasick again. He has to work during the few moments when he isn't feeling too poorly. Yesterday I came into our cabin at three in the afternoon, and there he stood in his nightshirt and cap, painting away.

Mid-June
Oakley

We landed at Bayou Sara this morning and walked the five miles to Oakley through the woods. Mr. A. started out scowling. He was unhappy again, all wrinkled brow and thin lips. How he hates the thought of being a tutor! "Waste of time," he fumes. "What is John James Audubon doing teaching drawing to a rich man's spoiled daughter when my birds are waiting for me?" But as we walked, I could see him growing more cheerful. It is not just that everything looks different here—the holly and beech trees and the magnolia and the tall oaks. Everything *smells* different as well. I have never sniffed such a variety of blossoms. Their fragrance hangs in the air and is so sweet it fairly make one dizzy. Many of the plants and flowers are entirely new to me. I must find out what they are and draw them. Oh, and the birds! So many different species!

By the time we arrived at Oakley Mr. Audubon was fairly dancing along the path.

The house itself is large. It is three stories tall and has porches and verandahs all around. Vines grow on trellises everywhere, and so many of them are in bloom that the whole place truly looks like a house made of flowers. The garden in the back and on the sides have much marble statuary in them, and there are lovely stone walls on their borders. I was overwhelmed by the beauty of the place.

Mr. Pirrie met us at the edge of the plantation grounds. He seems a pleasant man. Showed us our room, which is large and clean. I had hoped we would each have our own room. Mr. A. has some strange sleeping habits. If he gets an idea for a drawing in the middle of the night, he turns up the lamp and goes to work. It is sometimes hard to get a night's sleep with John James Audubon as your bedfellow!

Met Mrs. Pirrie shortly after. Seems *she* rules this roost. Miss Pirrie and her father both take orders from her. Miss Eliza Pirrie is about fifteen years old and charming. I could not take my eyes off her.

I think we shall be happy here.

The Red-Cockaded Woodpecker

We took our first real walk through the woods around Oakley today. Came upon two red-cockaded woodpeckers. They are black and white birds with a spot of red on their heads. We saw them in a tall pine tree, picking bugs out of the bark and calling to each other in large voices. Mr. Audubon wanted them alive, so he could watch them move. We wounded these two slightly on the wings, and Mr. Audubon grabbed them where they fell. Now we had a puzzle. Where should we put the two live birds while we finished our hunting? Finally, Mr. A. thought to put them in his hat. After he did this, every time we used our guns the birds in the hat would cry loudly.

By the time we got home one had died. But the other one seemed still very lively. We put it in a large wooden cage in our room. Let me tell, it is well-named *woodpecker!* It wasn't many minutes before the chips were flying and the bird had pecked its way out of the cage.

Our room has one wall of bare brick. The woodpecker ran up this wall and began to pick bugs from the cracks in the brick. As it ate, Mr. Audubon drew it. I left both of them very busy. The woodpecker seemed not at all bothered by the slight wound in its wing. Mr. Audubon is delighted that he can sketch the bird in its natural way of standing and pecking. "See, Joseph," he

says. "How much better this is than Wilson's stiff little profile."
(He is still comparing his work with Alexander Wilson's, even
though that poor gentleman has been dead seven years.)

When I came back later in the evening, Mr. Audubon was
putting the finishing touches to his drawing. I asked him if he
was going to let the bird go when he finished.

"But of course, Joseph," he said. "We cannot feed this bird
enough insects to keep it alive."

A few minutes later he opened the window. At first the woodpecker hesitated on the sill. Then it flew away, not much the worse
for having spent the day as a model for John James Audubon.

Partnership

This place seems to have a magic about it. Is it the gentle
air or the sweet smells or the graceful plants and trees? Or
maybe it is the birds, which are so plentiful that hardly a day
goes by that we do not find several species. Whatever it is, we
both are working at Oakley as we have never worked before.

Our day goes this way: In the morning I draw or hunt while
Mr. Audubon gives Miss Pirrie her lesson. He teaches her
drawing, also some music and lessons in making jewelry of
braided hair. I wish I could join them in these sessions. Often,
when I am in the house, I hear them laughing and talking
together in her room.

Miss Pirrie is ever so nice. She told me the other day,
"Joseph, you may call me Eliza." Mr. Audubon says I blushed
clear up to my scalp. He teases me a bit about Miss Eliza. I
should think I might tease *him*. He is the one laughing and joking with her every morning. And he a married man almost three
times her age. Sometime those French manners of his—and all
that hand kissing—*ugh!*

But to get back to our *work*. Each afternoon we draw until dinner time and then sometimes even after that. My drawing is getting better all the time. Mr. Audubon has let me do the plants for several of his bird paintings. Some of the ones we have worked on together are:

Hooded warbler
Bobolink
Yellow-throated vireo
Painted bunting
American redstart

Yes, Joseph Mason and John James Audubon are becoming quite a partnership.

My father would have been proud of me.

Sickness

I have been sick in bed with some kind of fever. It is the fever season in Louisiana, and everyone is worried that I am contagious. Especially, I am not allowed to get anywhere near Miss Eliza, who is frail. That makes me sad, as I look forward more each day to our talks. I am trying to grow a beard while I am sick to surprise her. So far no luck.

Mrs. Pirrie fusses over me, bringing me special puddings and such.

Mr. Pirrie also visited me. Mr. Pirrie is an interesting man. He loves birds and art and is very proud that Mr. Audubon is staying in his house. I like Mr. Pirrie.

He came to my room last night to tell me about Nero. Nero was Mr. Pirrie's pet sparrow hawk. When we went hunting he often flew along with us, and if we killed a bird that was too mangled to draw we threw it to the hawk, who caught it in midair. Nero also dearly loved bats and mice and would squeal with pleasure if one recently caught and still alive was offered to him.

Every night Nero came home to roost in the same spot, that spot being the inner part of a window sash in Mr. Pirrie's room.

Mr. Pirrie told me that Nero has been killed. And not by a hunter's gun or even another wild bird. He was killed by a *chicken* on the plantation. The hen was guarding her brood when bold Nero, thinking he owned the place, came swooping down on one of her babes. The hen went after him, with disastrous results. Mr. Audubon says this is one of the dangers of taming a wild bird. It loses its natural caution.

I hope I can be up and around by tomorrow. I shall miss Mrs. Pirrie's special puddings, but I miss my drawing even more.

Birds Alive

Lately Mr. Audubon seems to be inclined toward catching birds alive. I think the more we get to know these little creatures, the harder it is to shoot them. Yesterday, while I was still ailing, he brought back a slightly wounded little cypress swamp flycatcher, which he handled tenderly and sketched. The little fellow twittered around the room for a while, snapping at Mr. A.'s fingers whenever he tried to pick him up. But as the hours passed, the bird drooped, and we could not get it to eat. By evening it was so weak that we knew it could not survive. Mr.

Audubon finally killed it and put it in some whiskey to preserve it. We both felt for the little creature and wished it had lived.

This hot weather has brought out millions of bugs in the Louisiana bottom land. We see the evidence in our birds. I never realized how much a little bird can eat; we have counted *hundreds* of insects in the craw of a single flycatcher.

The other day Mr. Audubon and I invented a wonderful way to catch hummingbirds alive. There is a lovely trumpet vine on the verandah, which is often visited by hummingbirds. We poured a bit of wine into several of its flowers, then stepped inside the house to watch from the window. Soon a humming-bird came. It sipped from the wine-soaked calyx and in a few minutes was so drunk that we captured it easily!

August 18, 1821

The hummingbirds may be drunk on wine, but Mr. Audubon and I are drunk on something else. We are drunk on art—tipsy with it— intoxicated with our work. We draw like fiends, have completed ten more paintings, better than ever. I do some of the beaks and legs of birds, as well as the flower backgrounds.

August 21, 1821

Hot again. We look for amusement during these long, sultry summer days. Found it today in the form of a rattlesnake, which we caught and killed. It was about five and a half feet long, had ten rattles. Mr. Pirrie says it's called a canebrake rattler and is common to these parts. Gets its name from its habit of hiding in the stands of sugar cane. These snakes climb trees, which I never saw a rattler do in Ohio. Mr. Audubon already has the idea he will use the snake in a painting of mockingbirds. He will have the snake attacking the mockingbirds' nest. Another of Mr. Audubon's fine ideas!

We spent the whole day sketching the rattler. We have to be quick about it because it won't last long in this weather. That Mr. Audubon—he was actually complaining that Mrs. Pirrie won't let him keep a rattlesnake in the house alive! He told her that his wife let him keep live rattlesnakes in their house in Kentucky. "No wonder Mrs. Audubon is not anxious to join you here," was Mrs. Pirrie's reply. Mrs. Pirrie has a sharp tongue, but I was glad. I don't think I would be keen on sharing my room with a rattlesnake, even in the interests of John James Audubon's great book.

Mr. Audubon and I both drew the rattlesnake, and so did Miss Eliza, who worked alongside us almost the whole time. Mr. Audubon says this kind of drawing is the best practice for a student. We lifted the snake's jaws, peered into its mouth, counted its teeth, examined its scales. In truth there wasn't a part of that creature that wasn't made note of. I worked for sixteen hours, and although this activity may not be to the taste of some people, it was a wonderful day for me.

Part of my pleasure, I admit, was in being in the company of Miss Eliza.

Heat

Miserable weather. The heat gives me headaches. But there is also something in the air that has nothing to do with the heat. What is going on here? Miss Eliza is all fidgets and blushes. Mrs. Pirrie snaps at Mr. Audubon, and he pretends not to notice. Mr. Pirrie goes up to bed early. I have the same feeling that one gets in the woods just before a bad storm.

The air is heavy with *something;* that's sure.

Crisis

Well. Now the fat is in the fire. Miss Eliza's doctor (who I think is also her beau) has told Mrs. Pirrie that he does not think it is good for Miss Eliza to spend so much time in Mr. Audubon's company. Mrs. Pirrie has told Mr. Pirrie, who has told Mr. Audubon, who is *furious*. He raged around our room tonight, saying bitterly that the doctor is jealous of his time with Miss Eliza. I can understand that. I am jealous of Mr. Audubon myself. And I do think that he has given a little *too* much of his attention to the girl. Too much, that is, for a man who has a wife and family of his own. But I could not tell this to Mr. Audubon; his feelings would be hurt. He can't help being charming.

As for me, I am still allowed to see Miss Eliza. In fact, I see her more than I did before, which is most pleasant. But I do not think this situation is going to last, and I am extremely worried for the future.

Fired

Last night Mr. Pirrie called Mr. Audubon into the study. When they came out, Mr. A. was white as a lily and looked positively *sick*. I knew what had happened.

Yes. We have been asked to leave.

So. This is the end of it. No more walks in these enchanted gardens. No more picking flame lilies and yellow flag in the bayous. No more collecting and painting those wonderful birds and plants. All that is over. Over, too, are my pleasant talks with Miss Eliza.

"Miss Eliza," says Audubon, scornfully. "She is the cause of all my trouble. Whenever tragedy strikes, *cherchez la femme!*" (That means look for the woman.) Mr. Audubon is not being fair. If anyone asks my opinion, he brought this on himself.

But it's purely a shame, the way it has turned out. Our work was going so well here. And now we have to leave. And where will we go, is what I'd like to know. We have no money. What if the Pirries don't pay us for the time we have been here? They owe Audubon more than $100.

We are very uncomfortable here now. Meals are a torture. We all sit down together at table, and our eyes look at anything but one another. Mrs. Pirrie's sharp tongue jabs at Mr. A., and Mr. Pirrie is embarrassed. Eliza—well, Miss Eliza Pirrie is a big disappointment to me. She says nothing to defend Mr. Audubon. I find this shabby. How could I have once thought her nice? I certainly don't think so anymore.

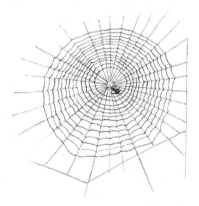

Good-bye, Oakley

Today we left Oakley. We're going back to New Orleans. Back to a rented room. Back to the portraits and the death masks and the pinching and scrimping to pay our rent.

The good-byes were painful. Mr. Pirrie was kind, but Mrs. Pirrie wasn't. Miss Eliza put out her hand for Mr. Audubon to kiss, but he ignored it. Good for him. Mrs. Pirrie offered me a suit of clothes that had belonged to her dead son, but Mr. Audubon wouldn't let me take it. He was probably right, but I do need clothes.

And so walked to the landing at Bayou Sara, perhaps for the last time. It was a painful parting. We were so happy at the plantation.

As we walked down the path, Mr. Audubon put his arm around me.

"Come, my young Sancho Panza," he said. "We will go on our way, tilting at more windmills."

I don't know what he meant by that. But when all is said and done, John James Audubon is probably a genius. So, windmills or birds, I will do what he asks of me.

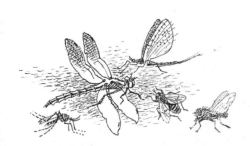

Part Four
Natchez
and Good-bye

October 30, 1821
Back in New Orleans

Here we are, back in New Orleans, where it is rainy and miserable. One full year has passed since we boarded the flatboat. Seems like a century.

"Joseph, it's time for us to take stock of ourselves." That's what Mr. Audubon said last night. So we have taken stock. We discover that we have completed sixty-two drawings and fifty portraits. In addition we have made hundreds of sketches of bees, butterflies, dragonflies, spiders, squirrels, rabbits, snakes, lizards, flowers, seeds, plants, trees, buds—and parts of animals, feet, claws, beaks, eyes. Believe me, if we have not drawn it, it is not worth a second glance.

As a result of all this labor, our total combined wealth is forty-two dollars. We have twenty-seven holes in our clothing (including boots and the seat of breeches) and a collection of bites, scratches, scars, scabs, burrs, thorns, and other tokens of our frontier life that would astonish a town dweller. We are much the worse for wear in every way.

Mr. Audubon has been trying to get a job as a teacher or dancing master—anything—but no one will have him. I am sure it is because of the way he looks. I heard someone say the other day, "Here comes that madman Audubon." Didn't tell Mr. A. this but advised him to get rid of that filthy suit and get himself some new clothes. So he has ordered a new garment, which will cost forty dollars and will take care of our "wealth."

"I didn't know that forty dollars could make a gentleman," says Mr. A. His tone is bitter.

Meanwhile, I am scouting about trying to collect old debts, like the one Mr. Heerman owes from when his wife took drawing lessons from Mr. A. I am getting skillful at this collecting trade—know how to keep my foot in a door. We've rented a room on the Rue St. Ann. Sixteen dollars a month. It's not worth five.

Work

Today Mr. A. got a teaching job with a family named Brand. He is to teach Mrs. Brand drawing at two dollars an hour. We also heard from someone that Mrs. Audubon and the boys are on their way here. Finally, after all this time, he has got her to give up her job and to come here. He is rushing around madly trying to get things ready for her.

Lucy

Mrs. Audubon and the boys have arrived. We have moved to larger quarters so we can all be under one roof.

I cannot tell here what a change has come over Mr. Audubon since his wife arrived. Truly, she *is* an extraordinary person. But his love for her is something extraordinary, too. When she comes into the room, he positively lights up. No wonder he was so eager for them to be together.

She brought all his paintings with her. Last night we sat by the fire going over them one by one. You can certainly see the steady progress of Mr. Audubon's work, especially since he is working more with watercolors instead of only with pastel and pencil, as he did earlier. But even the earlier work shows the mark of his gifted hand. He, of course, is never satisfied. "I remembered them as being better," he laments.

Another New Year

Another new year. It snowed on Christmas, and the ice was an inch thick when Mr. Rozier came to visit. Mr. Rozier is Mr. Audubon's former business partner and now very successful. Perhaps he is doing well because Mr. Audubon is no longer in the business with him?

We were snowed in but had a jolly time. It is good to be with *boys* for a change. Even though Victor and John Audubon are younger than I am, I enjoy their company. I have been with grownups too much the last year.

Mrs. Audubon is a very good cook, and we had a splendid Christmas dinner of stuffed goose and gravy. Part of the thanks for the meal goes to Mr. Audubon's trusty double-barreled shotgun. I covet that gun; I really do.

Our house always smells of cooking and baking now. And having Mrs. Audubon around has awakened all my longing for home. I don't think I can stay here much longer, even though Mr. Audubon has made a resolution to do ninety-nine birds in ninety-nine days. He claims he needs me still, but my thoughts are going more and more toward Ohio.

Neither of us was able to afford a new journal for this year, which explains why I am writing this on paper that was used to wrap some paint brushes. Mr. A. doesn't write at all these days. He is too busy with his teaching and his birds. I hope he doesn't make himself sick with such a heavy schedule. He complains of headache and of eyestrain all the time but won't quit. So since I can do no less when he is working so hard, we both end up working like demons.

A Mr. Gilbert now brings us birds, so we do not have to spend the time hunting them. But he must be paid. So Mr. Audubon still makes portraits. Recently we did a portrait of Don Antonio de Sedella, a local priest. Mr. Audubon painted the head, and I painted the body, but of course no one knows that. It was sold as Mr. Audubon's work. It would be nice to get some of the credit for my labor.

Mr. Audubon has *promised* me that my name will remain on the drawings when the engravings are finally made for *The Birds of America*.

Good-bye Again to Lucy

Mrs. Brand is pregnant and is not going to continue her lessons. We thought for a while that we were going to lose our livelihood, but the Brands have now hired Mrs. Audubon as a companion. She and the boys will live with them at their plantation until the baby is born. As for Mr. Audubon and me, we will set sail once again, this time on the ship *éclat*. We are going back up to Natchez, for we seem to have no more work in New Orleans.

Once again we are paying our passage with crayon portraits of the captain and his wife.

I wonder how Mrs. Audubon feels about always having to earn a living. Once I heard her say to him, "You know, John, you can charm the birds from the trees, but that won't put food in your children's bellies."

Another Crisis

Does it ever end? A week ago when we came on board this ship Mr. Audubon opened his sea chest and discovered that a cask of gunpowder had exploded in it. The gunpowder has stained the drawings beyond repair. I think almost half of all his new paintings have been ruined. This event has so depressed him that he has taken to his bed. He will do nothing but lie there and stare at the wall. Each day I feed him and tend him as he needs me, but he refuses to get up. It has been four days, and I do not know anything more to do for him. I fear Mr. Audubon is losing his mind.

Is this bird mania finally to end by killing him, as it did Alexander Wilson? Everyone knows that great naturalist died of dysentery, contracted after he went into the water to rescue a wounded bird. And will this one die of heartbreak over pictures of birds?

Working Again

I knew only that I had to get him out of his desperate mood. So every day for the past three days I set up my drawing board where he could watch me. I did not say anything; I simply drew and painted. Today for the first time I saw that he was watching me. And after a while he said, "No, Joseph, not that way. More design, more *esprit*." A little while later he got up to show me. Just what I had hoped for. And he has been drawing ever since. Praise heaven! Mr. Audubon is working again!

April 4

Spring is here. We were invited for hunting on a plantation nearby. Had fine shooting and then dined on the roasted eggs of a softshell turtle. There is no finer meal than that. Pleasant day; Mr. Audubon is his old jovial self.

And yet—and yet—I have the strangest feeling that our time together is growing short. I am truly homesick for Ohio. But when I mention it to Mr. Audubon, he folds his lips tightly and says nothing. I cannot press him. But one day soon I shall have to.

School

We are staying in Natchez, and Mr. Audubon has got a job teaching at a fancy school in the neighboring town of Washington. It's not what he wants to do, but again, he must.

Summer Heat

When summer comes to Natchez, Mississippi, the air grows still. And what was in spring a sweet scent of flowers and rich earth in summer becomes rotted and stinking. In Natchez-under-the-Hill, where the poor live, it is filthy beyond description. The water sits in muddy pools, and the insects breed and drive us nearly mad.

At the plantations they close the shutters against the midday sun and the servants fan their masters with palmetto fans. Some people leave and go on holiday to a cooler place. Those who stay nap in the afternoons and sit on their verandahs, sipping cool drinks.

But in the room of John James Audubon and Joseph Mason, we do none of these things. We work and work and work some more. Like carthorses. And Mr. Audubon walks to Washington every day in the heat, to teach his classes and then comes back to work again and endlessly on birds, *birds*, BIRDS!

I want to go home. I really want to go home. I must go home. Tonight I will ask him.

Fever

When Mr. Audubon came home last night, he was so pale I didn't have the heart to ask him anything. He went straight to bed and this morning was unable to get up. He sweats and shakes, and I know those signs. He has the fever, the dreaded disease of this place. Each year hundreds, maybe thousands, of people die of it.

I have sent for Dr. Provan, who is a friend of the family.

Mr. Audubon worse. Dr. Provan stayed the night.

Mr. Audubon very weak. I have sent word to Mrs. Audubon.

Oh God, is he going to die? After all he has been through, will he die? Dr. Provan will tell me nothing, but what I see is that John James Audubon is shivering and sweating himself to death.

Better

At last. He is better. Thin and pale, but better. Mrs. Audubon couldn't come because Mrs. Brand was near death too. But she sent the boys, who will be going to school here.

Something has happened to Mr. Audubon since his illness.

He is calmer, more thoughtful. He has decided that he will become a portrait artist and will give up his birds. I cannot believe it; it is as if when the illness passed, his bird fever passed too.

So I have got my wish. I am going home. But I did not figure that all the work we did together would be in vain. It will be a *sin* if those bird paintings never get published. That's what I say, a sin.

One Last Trip

Today we took our last trip together. Went out in a bayou, just the two of us. We went in a pirogue that we had bought in Louisiana. Pirogues are those wonderful little boats hollowed out of a cypress log. They can get into places where no other kind of boat can go. In Louisiana there is a saying that you can float on a heavy dew in a pirogue.

And so we paddled through the bayou—past cypress knees and lily pads and through watery fields of pennywort. Mr. Audubon never raised his gun today, nor did I. It was as if my teacher were giving me this day to be quietly among my wild friends and to say good-bye.

I saw a green snake slither along the top of the water. I reached down and grabbed it, held it for a moment. It's skin was cool against my hand. Then I let it go.

The birds twittered and fluttered above our heads, so many of the ones we had already committed to paper: warblers and flycatchers and the long-legged wading birds that Mr. Audubon loves so much—ibises and spoonbills and herons. They were all there today.

Around dusk we came to a lake. My friend said, "Joseph, let us stay and have our supper here."

"What supper?" I asked, because we had no means to get a meal without our guns.

Then Mr. Audubon reached into his pocket and pulled out a blowgun made of cane, which had in it a sharp arrow. He said he had learned how to make these from the Choctaw Indians. Scarcely fifteen minutes later he had stunned a wild duck with it, and the bird was roasting in our fire.

When our bellies were full, we sat on the shore, listening to the tree frogs' chorus and watching the flying squirrels perform their acrobatic leaps among the trees. Once a bull alligator bellowed, and we heard the tail of a beaver slap the water.

Mr. Audubon sat quietly, letting me have my fill of the woods. Letting me say my good-byes. And I did say them. Good-bye to the wild orchids. Good-bye to Spanish moss, to great clumsy alligators and to the delicate little warblers, to the frogs and snakes and all the forms of wildlife that John James Audubon and I shared with each other.

And so today we parted. He cried. I wanted to. He gave me his double-barreled shotgun. He gave me chalks and paints and brushes and paper, so I can work my way home. But this is not the half of it. The biggest things John James Audubon gave me are not things I carry in my bag. They are images I will carry forever in my head and my heart.

So good-bye, John James Audubon. Thank you for everything. I hope that you will never give up your dream.

January 30, 1838

It is now eighteen years since I made the trip with John James Audubon.

Today I learned that the last engraving of Audubon's work has been made. He did it; he finished *The Birds of America*

Folio and a five-volume book, called *Ornithological Biographies,* to accompany it. I understand that he is the toast of England. Both here and abroad people are clamoring to buy a complete set of the folio for $1,000.

It is just as I thought it would be. John James Audubon has become famous. But a genius is not without his faults. I can never quite forgive him for taking my name off the paintings we did together. I know that often artists do not credit their assistants. But a promise is a promise. And after all, I *did* do the flowers and plants for 50 of the 435 plates.

Are all geniuses scoundrels, I wonder? Oh, let it be, I tell myself. For after all, I have my life here in Philadelphia. I am a portrait painter and well known for it. Perhaps I owe that to John James Audubon.

Our lives will never touch again. But for a little while we were almost as close as father and son. I will try to remember only those good times. And to think kindly of the man with whom I shared so many frontier adventures.

A NOTE FROM THE AUTHOR

Although his journal is my creation, Joseph Mason himself was a real boy. I first learned about him from the legend under an Audubon painting at the New York Historical Society. It indicated that Joseph Mason had done the flower background for some of Audubon's work and that he was thirteen years old at the time.

My interest aroused, I began to look for other confirmation of the fact that Audubon had had a young assistant. I found it, in all the Audubon biographies. Joseph Mason did indeed exist. John James Audubon *was* his drawing teacher. And they *had* traveled together down the Mississippi and Ohio for eighteen months.

But the acknowledgments of Joseph's existence were no more than tantalizing glimpses. A few pages. Nothing more. It was not until I located an unedited diary of Audubon's travels during 1820 and 1821 that a picture of Audubon and Joseph began to emerge. There, in Audubon's own words, was a detailed account of their daily life—the hunting for birds, the hard times, the endless hours of drawing. And the good times, too—the dinners in New Orleans, the hikes, the beauty of the Pirrie plantation where they stayed. And through it all, the thread of this extraordinary friendship and collaboration.

Using the journal as a factual base, I began to write a new journal—Joseph's journal. I looked to other Audubon biographies for reference, particularly Alice Ford's *John James Audubon*. And I drew on other Audubon writings, especially the *Ornithological Biographies*, in which Audubon describes in detail both the behavior and his experiences with each bird he painted.

The result is a story as "true" as I could make it. Almost every incident in this book actually happened. Although the conversations are fictional, they are based on facts about Audubon and Joseph as revealed in the above sources or in Joseph Mason's statements later in his life.

I'm indebted to a number of people who helped me, notably: Ruth Hand of the Pearl River Public Library, who located the diary without which there would have been no story; my husband, Fred Brenner, whose unique perspective on Audubon through his own work as a wildlife artist added so much to my understanding; and Barbara Lalicki, my editor, whose marvelous enthusiasm for this project was a source of inspiration and reinforcement.